OH!

WORDS BY KEVIN HENKES
PICTURES BY LAURA DRONZEK

GREENWILLOW BOOKS, NEW YORK

For Will and Clara

Acrylic paints were used for the full-color art.
The text type is Italia Book.

Text copyright © 1999 by Kevin Henkes
Illustrations copyright © 1999 by Laura Dronzek

Printed in Singapore by Tien Wah Press
First Edition 10 9 8 7 6 5 4 3 2 1

Library of Congress Cataloging-in-Publication Data
Henkes, Kevin.
Oh! / by Kevin Henkes ;
illustrated by Laura Dronzek.
   · p.   cm.
Summary: The morning after a snowfall
finds animals and children playing.
ISBN 0-688-17053-6 (trade)
ISBN 0-688-17054-4 (lib. bdg.)
[1. Snow—Fiction.   2. Animals—Play behavior—
Fiction.   3. Play—Fiction.   4. Stories in rhyme.]
I. Dronzek, Laura, ill.   II. Title.   PZ8.3.H4165Oh
1999   [E]—dc21   98-51890   CIP   AC

The snow falls and falls all night.

In the morning everything is white.

And everyone wants to play.

Oh!

The squirrel wants to play.

Skitter, skitter, skitter,

quick gray squirrel.

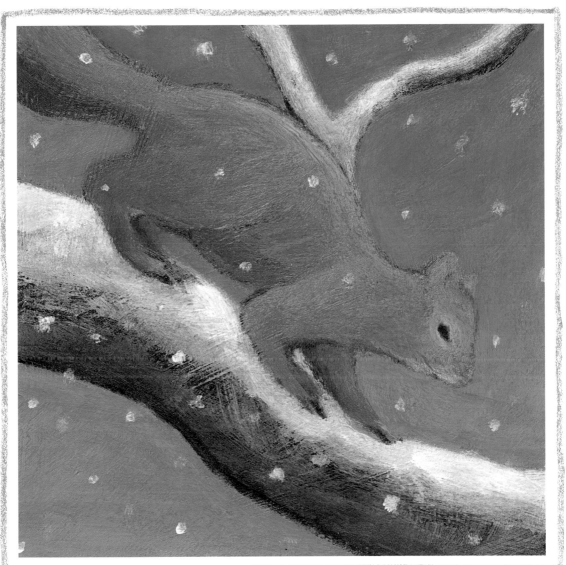

The rabbit wants to play.

Hop, hop, hop,

shy little rabbit.

The cat wants to play.

Sneak, sneak, sneak,

brave young cat.

The dog wants to play.
Run, run, run,
clever old dog.

The children want to play.

Jump, jump, jump,

fat bouncy children.

The birds want to play, too—

up in the air like snowflakes falling.

OH!

In the afternoon they play again.

And then . . .

The sky grows dark.

The snow turns blue.

Playtime is over

for you

and you

and you

and you

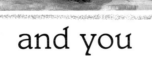

and you

and you.

Rush on home.

Good-bye, snow.

See you again tomorrow.

Oh!